Betty the Yeti
AND THE FIRST DAY OF SCHOOL

by Mandy R Marx

illustrated by Antonella Fant

raintree
a Capstone company — publishers for children

Raintree is an imprint of Capstone Global Library Limited, a company incorporated in England and Wales having its registered office at 264 Banbury Road, Oxford, OX2 7DY – Registered company number: 6695582

www.raintree.co.uk
myorders@raintree.co.uk

Designed by Hilary Wacholz
Original illustrations © Capstone Global Library Limited 2024
Originated by Capstone Global Library Ltd

978 1 3982 5260 8

British Library Cataloguing in Publication Data
A full catalogue record for this book is available from the British Library.

Printed and bound in India.

CONTENTS

MEET BETTY AND HER FAMILY

Betty Yeti and her family moved from a cold mountain home to an apartment in the city. Mama Yeti, Betty and her twin brothers, Eddy and Freddy, are the only yetis in town. Getting used to a new place is hard. But it's especially hard when you're a yeti who isn't quite ready to stand out.

Mama

Eddy

Betty

Freddy

Chapter 1

MORNING JITTERS

"I'm so excited about school!" said Cecilia. "Aren't you, Betty?"

Betty Yeti felt a lump in her throat. "No," she said, "I'm scared."

It was the Yetis' first day at a *new* school.

Cecilia knew Betty felt shy sometimes.

"Don't worry, Betty," said Cecilia. "Our school is fun!"

"I'm just afraid no one will like me because I'm . . . different," Betty said.

"That's what makes you wonderful," said Cecilia.

Chapter 2

FITTING IN

Betty and Cecilia walked into their classroom. The other children stared. Their mouths dropped. They had never seen a yeti before.

Betty's heart thumped. She didn't like everyone looking at her.

"Sit by me, Betty," said Cecilia.

Betty looked at the desk
by Cecilia. It looked small.
Would she fit?

"Everyone, please take your
seats," said their teacher.
"My name is Mr Cyrus."

Betty squeezed into her desk
as Mr Cyrus wrote his name
on the board.

"Please draw a picture of who you live with," said Mr Cyrus. "I'll hang the pictures around our classroom!"

Betty liked to draw. But her joy
soon turned to sadness. The paper
was white. So was Betty's family.
A white crayon didn't show up on
white paper. Betty wanted to cry.

Betty felt too shy to ask
for help.

"Psst!" Betty heard suddenly.
"Do you want some black
paper?" asked the boy sitting
next to her.

"Thanks," she said. "I'm Betty."

"I'm Cael," he said. "White crayon will show up better on black paper."

Cael seemed nice. Betty felt a bit better.

Chapter 3

A STICKY SITUATION

The rest of the morning passed quickly. Betty almost forgot her nerves.

The bell rang. Time for lunch!

Mr Cyrus excused the class. Everyone got out of their seats – everyone but Betty.

"Aren't you coming, Betty?" asked Mr Cyrus.

"I . . . I'm trying," said Betty.

"Is something wrong?" asked Mr Cyrus.

"I'm stuck!" cried an embarrassed Betty.

Betty was upset. "I'm sorry.
I'm just so much bigger than
everyone else."

"There's nothing wrong
with your size," said Mr Cyrus.
"Being different is wonderful.
How boring would it be if
we were all the same?"

Betty gave him a little smile.

"I should have known a yeti would need a different desk," he said. "I'll get you out. Let me get some tools."

Mr Cyrus left and came
back with tools. He took apart
Betty's desk.

"Hmmm," Mr Cyrus said.
He went to the reading corner
and grabbed a pillow. "If you
sat on a pillow, would this table
be the right height, Betty?"

Betty tried the pillow. It was
cosy. She liked it better than
a chair.

Chapter 4

A STRONG CASE FOR BEING DIFFERENT

Betty was late to lunch.

Everyone was playing already.

Betty ate alone and went out

to the playground. She couldn't

see Cecilia or Cael.

Betty sat down near the

roundabout. She had

no one to play with.

Then she heard a boy say,
"I'm tired. I don't want to push
the roundabout anymore."

"But who will push us?"
asked another boy.

Betty perked up. She wasn't
just big. She was strong.

"I'll do it!" she said, giving them a giant push.

The children cheered and yelled, "Yay! Betty the Yeti!"

Betty grinned. Maybe being different was wonderful after all.

Glossary

embarrass feel silly or foolish in front of others

height how tall something is

jitters extremely nervous

thump pound; your heart pounds when it is beating faster and louder

yeti large, furry ape-like creature that may or may not exist in cold, faraway places

Talk about it

1. Betty was nervous about being different from the other kids. Have you ever felt different from other people? Did it make you nervous? Why or why not?

2. Betty was embarrassed when she got stuck in her desk. Has anything embarrassing ever happened to you? What did you do and how did you handle it?

3. Betty realized that her large size meant she was stronger than the other children. Do you have any skills that make you stand out?

Write about it

1. Cecilia told Betty that their school was fun. What would the most fun school you could imagine look like? Draw a picture of it and point out what makes it fun.

2. Betty was new at school, but so were her brothers, Eddy and Freddy. How do you think their first day at a new school went? Write a short story about it.

3. Mr Cyrus tried to show Betty that he cared about hcr. Write about a time a teacher was kind to you. How did that make you feel?

About the author

Mandy R Marx is a writer and editor. She lives in a chilly town in Minnesota, USA, with her husband, daughter and a white, silky haired pup. She has a curious mind and stays on the lookout for yetis. In her spare time, Mandy enjoys singing, laughing with friends and family and walking her pup through what she suspects is a magical forest.

About the illustrator

María Antonella Fant is a visual designer, children's book illustrator and concept artist. Her illustrations reflect her childish, restless and curious personality, taking inspiration from animated cartoons and children's books from her childhood. María enjoys the way a child thinks, drawing like them and for them. María was born, and currently lives, in Argentina.